3/05

## Moon Magic

A Magical World Awaits You
Read

THE SECRETS OF DROON

#1: The Hidden Stairs and the Magic Carpet

#2: Journey to the Volcano Palace

#3: The Mysterious Island

#4: City in the Clouds

#5: The Great Ice Battle

#6: The Sleeping Giant of Goll

#7: Into the Land of the Lost

#8: The Golden Wasp

#9: The Tower of the Elf King

#10: Quest for the Queen

#11: The Hawk Bandits of Tarkoom

#12: Under the Serpent Sea

#13: The Mask of Maliban

#14: Voyage of the *Jaffa Wind*

#15: The Moon Scroll

#16: The Knights of Silversnow

Special Edition #1: The Magic Escapes

#17: Dream Thief

#18: Search for the Dragon Ship

#19: The Coiled Viper

#20: In the Ice Caves of Krog

#21: Flight of the Genie

Special Edition #2: Wizard or Witch?

#22: The Isle of Mists

#23: The Fortress of the Treasure Queen

#24: The Race to Doobesh

#25: The Riddle of Zorfendorf Castle

Special Edition #3: Voyagers of the Silver Sand

#26: The Moon Dragon

#27: The Chariot of Queen Zara

#28: In the Shadow of Goll

Special Edition #4: Sorcerer

#29: Pirates of the Purple Dawn

#30: Escape from Jabar-Loo

#31: Queen of Shadowthorn

Special Edition #5: Moon Magic

and coming soon

#32: The Treasure of the Orkins

# THE SECRETS OF DROON

— TONY ABBOTT —

## Moon Magic

Illustrated by David Merrell
Cover illustration by Tim Jessell

SCHOLASTIC INC.
New York  Toronto  London  Auckland  Sydney
Mexico City  New Delhi  Hong Kong  Buenos Aires

To My Family,
Past, Present,
and To Come

For more information about the continuing saga of Droon,
please visit Tony Abbott's website at
www.tonyabbottbooks.com

ISBN-13: 978-0-439-90255-7
ISBN-10: 0-439-90255-X

12 11 10 9 8 7 6 5 4 3 2 1          8 9 10 11 12 13/0

Printed in the U.S.A.
First printing, February 2008

# Contents

1. Wayfarers All      1

2. The Magical Grove of Magic      16

3. To the Blue Flame      31

4. The Moon and the Smoke      49

5. Burned by Silver Fire      61

6. Hand to Hand      72

7. Palace of Smoke      81

8. And . . . They're Off!      90

9. The Dark Future      99

10. Under the Black Palace      116

11. The Magic of the Moon      136

12. A Very Good Thing      149

# One

## Wayfarers All

"*Salamandra, no!*" Eric Hinkle shouted as he tumbled head over heels into the roaring time tunnel known as the Portal of Ages. "Stop the Portal now!"

But the thorn queen wouldn't stop it. "Sorry, Eric. No can do. You're all on quests now. Two of you in the past, two in the future. Have fun!"

"No more riddles!" Eric shouted. "No more puzzles!"

"That's it!" said Salamandra. "Pretend it's a really big puzzle. Then put it all together. You just may save Droon!"

"But what does that mean?"

"Buh-bye!" she said, smiling crookedly. With a twist of her magic staff, Eric and his friends Julie, Keeah, and Neal went hurtling into the coiling, whirling storm of darkness.

"Hey, hey, whoaaaa!" Neal shouted, zooming past Eric in one direction while Julie flew by in another.

Laughing at the top of her lungs, Salamandra flicked her wrist, and Eric was sucked toward a side tunnel. Bracing himself for an instant, he thought back to five minutes earlier.

Five crazy minutes earlier . . .

They had all been on a mountaintop in the magical world of Droon. He, Princess Keeah, Julie, and Neal had just battled

Gethwing, the terrifying four-winged dragon, when Salamandra conjured her magical Portal of Ages.

The Portal's spinning storm connected times and places in Droon and in Eric's home, the Upper World.

With a simple turn of her magic staff, Salamandra could have thrown Gethwing far into the past with no chance of ever returning.

Instead, she stood by as the dragon heaved the children one by one into the Portal. Then she stirred them around the whirling time-storm, laughing and laughing.

Had she betrayed them?

At first, Eric thought so.

But at the last second, Salamandra let Eric drag Gethwing into the Portal with him. Then she told him a magic word he did not understand.

*Reki-ur-set.*

Eric pleaded that he no longer understood ancient words. But Salamandra said the word wasn't in an ancient language.

It was in his own language.

*Reki-ur-set?*

*What did it mean? Was it a riddle?*

Of course it was a riddle. Salamandra was the queen of riddles. She had sent Eric visions and clues for a long time. He barely understood any of them. One thing he did understand, however, was that Salamandra had taken his wizard powers away. On a recent adventure, he had used her magic staff to save his friends. The price he paid was losing every single power he had.

Now, as he struggled not to get hurled away to some distant time and place, Eric stared into Salamandra's eyes.

They were cold and cruel.

They were mysterious.

And yet . . . she had told him things.

*You're all on quests now. . . .*

"Eric, watch out!" Keeah cried suddenly. "Gethwing's right behind you!"

Eric jerked his head and saw the giant moon dragon lunging through the time tunnel straight at him. "Nooo —"

"Enough!" shouted Salamandra. She stirred her magic staff, and three quick blasts of wind tore Keeah, Gethwing, and Eric in different directions.

Before Eric could think of what to do — *whoosh!* — darkness engulfed him, and he fell, fell, fell, until he couldn't fall anymore.

*PLOP!*

Eric landed on solid ground, quickly but softly, as if he had fallen out of bed.

"Oh . . . whoa . . ."

Opening his eyes, he saw a spiral of thorns whirl briefly in the dark sky above him, then fade to nothing. The Portal of Ages — Salamandra's magical time tunnel — had disappeared.

Eric sat up.

Everything around him was gray, as if bathed in the last stages of twilight. The landscape reminded him of an old black-and-white photograph. It looked like the surface of the moon.

Focusing as best as he could, Eric determined that he was on a low ridge over a plain of dark earth that stretched for miles in every direction. In the far distance he could see a range of tall black peaks arching up toward the sky.

Nearby lay a large swamp filled with water the color of oil. Its shore was thick with reeds.

"Nice," he commented. "Where am I? Nowhere?"

He tried to remember all the remote

places he had ever learned about in school. The deserts in China. The southern tip of South America. The North Pole.

This didn't look like any of them.

Eric struggled to his feet and yelled at the top of his lungs, "Hey! Neal? Keeah? Julie? Anyone? Answer me!"

He paused and listened.

There was no response.

Eric wandered over to the swamp and peered in. All he saw was his face surrounded by nothing. He felt like burying his head in his hands. He didn't want to be there. He didn't want to be anywhere except at the gates of Jaffa City.

He knew that at that very moment Emperor Ko, the foul leader of the beasts, was leading his armies to the royal capital to burn it down.

Eric wanted to help defend Keeah's beautiful city. Even though he'd lost his powers, he could still fight the beasts. And he *would* fight them, until he breathed his last.

"Fine," he said aloud. "I'm on my own —"

*Whooooo . . .*

He heard a faraway sound. At first it was low, then it grew louder, as if it were coming closer.

"I don't like that sound," Eric said, staring into the distance. "I think I'd better —"

"I think you'd better *shhhh*!" hissed a voice.

Eric whirled around to face the swamp again. A head was sticking up out of the black water.

"Get in here, Eric!"

He looked closer. The head had a crown on it. "Keeah? Is that you? Why are you in —"

"Get in here!" Keeah said. She jumped out of the water, slapped her hand over his mouth, and dragged him back into the swamp with her.

"Now breathe through this reed and hide under the surface," she ordered. "He's coming!"

"What? Who's coming —"

Keeah stuck a reed in Eric's mouth and — *splash!* — pushed his head under the water.

As Eric tried to suck air through the reed and not get water up his nose, Keeah sank down next to him. She pointed up through the water at the black sky above them.

And there he was.

Gethwing. The moon dragon.

In the same place and time as him and Keeah!

The dragon's four black wings moved slowly through the heavy air. Gethwing's fiery red eyes scoured the land below as if

searching for something. He circled the swamp twice, then flew on over the plains.

Not able to last another second under-water, Eric shot through the surface and breathed out. "Pah! That is so gross!"

"Believe me," said Keeah, bobbing up next to him, "if there was another way, I'd have done it. But from the moment the Portal dropped me here, I felt him nearby. He's looking for something . . . or someone —"

Another sound broke the quiet.

*Ah-roo . . . ah-roo . . .*

It sounded like a wolf howling from the distant mountain peaks. The howl faded as quickly as it had begun.

"I've decided," said Eric. "I don't like it here."

"This is no part of Droon I've ever

seen," Keeah said, twirling on her heels to dry her clothes and hair. "I hate not knowing where we are."

Eric felt the same. "Maybe there are clues we're not seeing. I'll climb the ridge and try to get a better view."

As he clambered up the top of the nearby ridge, Eric couldn't get the image of Ko's army out of his mind. It was the largest force of torch-wielding beasts he had ever seen.

He knew that while he and the other kids were falling into the Portal, Galen was flying to defend Jaffa City. But he doubted that even the wizard had magic enough to stop Ko's vicious attack.

As Eric scanned from the ridge, Keeah took a closer look at the strange, hard earth all around them. Her fall from the stormy Portal had been fast, but she wasn't hurt. She remembered seeing Eric look so small and helpless amid the giant stones.

She knew he hurt without his powers.

*Powers!*

Keeah's heart quaked to remember how her parents, King Zello and Queen Relna, rode swiftly to defend their home. Did they have any chance of defeating Ko? Would they be hurt in the battle to come? What would she find when she returned to the present?

"Nothing," said Eric, returning from the ridge. "Nothing, that is, except for that tiny blue light. Over there. On the tip of that mountain." He pointed to a dark, jagged mountaintop far away. "Can you see it?"

Keeah stood in front of him, scanning the distance. "Uh . . . no . . ."

Eric put his hands on her shoulders and moved her slightly. "There. It looks like it's in a cave."

Keeah looked and looked, squinting with all her might, but she didn't see anything. "You must have really good eyesight."

Eric breathed deeply. "Maybe. Anyway, Salamandra said we're on a quest. If we're supposed to go somewhere and find something, maybe we should go toward that light."

Keeah nodded. "With any luck, we'll find out what our quest is. And where Julie and Neal are. And how to save Jaffa City."

*And maybe what 'Reki-ur-set' means!* thought Eric.

Another eerie call pierced the air. *Whoooo!*

"Gethwing's circling back," said Keeah.

"Okay, but no more swamps," said Eric.

Keeah smiled. "I agree. Let's do something basic here. Let's run!"

"I like it," said Eric. "To the mountain!"

As they charged across the black earth, trying to stay clear of Gethwing, Eric and Keeah wondered the same thing: Were their friends together, and did they know where they were? And *when* they were?

# Two

## The Magical Grove of Magic

Neal's first thought as he fell from the Portal of Ages was that his turbaned head was the most padded part of him.

His second thought was that he didn't want to land on his head.

Quick as a wink, Neal whipped off his turban, stretched it wide, and sat in it.

Then he screamed. "Ahhhhhh —"

Then he landed. *Thump!*

"Uh . . . oww?"

His fall was fast, but his landing was soft. Realizing he wasn't hurt, Neal bounced to his feet, wrapped the turban of midnight-blue silk back around his head, and looked around.

He was in a forest, and it was night.

Lush green plants grew up on every side. Vines coiled down from tall trees whose leaves drooped and swayed. Everything was dappled with bright, silver moonlight.

He closed his eyes and tried to remember how he had gotten there. In his mind he saw a half-dozen pizzas floating around, a big bowl of macaroni and cheese, three giant pickles, a half-eaten peanut butter sandwich, and the face of Salamandra, Queen of Shadowthorn.

"Oh, her!" said Neal. "Now I remember.

I got thrown into her Portal of Ages. So I landed here in a forest. A forest that is really beautifuuu — uuuff!"

Something heavy dropped onto his back, and he slammed to the ground face-first.

"Thanks for the soft landing!" said a familiar voice.

Neal rolled over and saw Julie standing over him, brushing herself off.

He grumbled, "Sure, sure. Glad I could help."

Julie pulled him to his feet, then went still. She listened as a breeze played among the high branches. The leaves tinkled like chimes.

"This place," she whispered. "It seems . . . I don't know . . ."

"Magical?" Neal added. "I know. Which totally makes sense, because Salamandra sent us here. We're on a quest. I love quests!"

"But a quest for what?" asked Julie.

She knew — they all knew — that even though Salamandra loved riddles and mysteries and secrets and quests and journeys, there was usually a reason behind them.

"The question is . . . did she send us to Droon or the Upper World?" she said.

Neal frowned. "It's magical, so probably Droon. Right?"

But Julie knew that the Upper World — *their* world — was once home to its own brand of astonishing magic. The wizard Galen, his brothers Urik and Sparr, and their mother, Queen Zara, had all been born in the Upper World long ago.

Over the years, magic had nearly disappeared from the Upper World. That was partly the fault of Salamandra, who stole magic in her younger days. Part of it was the passing of time itself.

*So,* Julie thought, *could this be our world?*

Neal sniffed. The air smelled like apples baking in an oven. "I read somewhere that traveling in time makes you really hungry."

Julie gave him a look. "While you think about food, I'll try to figure out where we are and why we're here —"

Trees rustled suddenly behind them.

Turning quickly, the two friends spied something hazy moving among the trees. The thing was the size and shape of a giant, but it made no sound of its own. And though they could see the leaves on the trees flutter as the thing passed, they could not see the thing itself.

"Why am I suddenly afraid?" asked Julie.

"Because you're smart?" said Neal. He realized that the fragrance of apples baking had been replaced by the heavy odor of smoke. "Phew," he murmured.

"That's no woodland creature," said Julie. "It smells like a fire. We need to follow it."

"Or we could run in the opposite direction," said Neal. "That's an option." Julie narrowed her eyes at him. "Or not. Your idea is good, too."

"Then let's go," she said, peering through the heavy growth of trees. "But not on the ground. Let's follow it from the treetops."

Neal broke into a grin. Flying was one of his favorite genie powers. "I like how you think. Or even *that* you think!"

"At least one of us should," Julie retorted.

Together the two friends leaped into

the trees and flitted from one branch to another, following the thing through the woods below.

But the forest was vast and dense. The faster they flew, the more lost they got. Stopping finally, they realized that the being, whatever it was, was either gone or hiding.

"Now what?" asked Neal. "I don't smell smoke anymore. It's more like . . . like . . ." He sniffed. "Baked apples again. This way!"

Together, the two flew on until they squeezed through a thicket of vines and tumbled into a grove of leafy apple trees.

Bright silver moonlight played upon the trees' fragrant white blossoms.

The moon shone full on them like a silver spotlight. In the middle of the grove was a perfectly round white stone. There was a circular indentation the size of a small saucer in the center of the stone.

Flames licked the sides of the stone from a fire pit underneath, making the stone seem like an anvil. There were tools scattered all around it.

"I can't believe it!" whispered Julie.

"You found the baked apples?" said Neal.

"No. I think that maybe . . . this is our world," she said. "A moonlit grove. An anvil. Tools. What does this make you think of?"

Neal closed his eyes. Among the floating pizzas, there were now several bowls of cereal and a single silver disk beaming with light.

His eyes popped open. "Wait. A round silver thing? The Moon Medallion? Are you saying that we're, like, five hundred years ago?"

The ancient and powerful Moon Medallion had been created by Queen Zara before the world of Droon had been discovered. It contained all of the queen's vast and powerful wizard magic.

Julie searched the grove for other clues, then stopped. "Oh . . ."

"Oh?" Neal turned to her. "Oh . . . what?"

Julie gulped. "Oh . . . *her*."

A woman had entered the grove. She was dressed in a silver gown and wore a silver diadem around her head. She was armored from neck to waist with a tunic of hammered silver.

It was Zara, the Queen of Light.

Both Neal and Julie realized at once that they had arrived in the Upper World before Emperor Ko had attacked and kidnapped Zara and her youngest son, Sparr.

As Julie bowed, her mind raced. "Queen Zara, we've never met before. We are from . . . five hundred years in the future. I'm Julie. This is Neal."

Zara gazed into their eyes. "I think you are friends. . . ."

Julie nodded. "We hope so."

Neal tried to sort out in his mind how time twisted and turned and how he could be back before he was born, but all he saw were pickles and macaroni, so he gave up.

"Something called the Portal of Ages threw us here," he told Zara. "Our friends Eric and Keeah are probably in different places and times, and we're all on quests, only we don't know what —"

All of a sudden, the leaves rustled, and a young boy swung down on a vine and landed in front of Julie and Neal.

"Who goes there?" he demanded.

The boy looked nearly their age and wore a cape of deep blue with stars and moons on it. He carried a short, curved staff in one hand.

Neal gasped. "Whoa . . . are you Galen?"

The boy grinned. "You've heard of me?"

"Uh . . ."

"Was it the flood I stopped single-handedly?" the boy asked eagerly. "Or did you hear about me and the seven-headed tree-dwarf? The Backward Clock of Time? The Waterfall of Fiery Blades? You really can't believe some of the stories they tell about me. You can believe *all* of them! I'm writing them down in a book I call the *Galen Chronicles*."

"It's a fantasy!" said an older boy, bounding through the trees. It was Urik, the eldest of Zara's three sons. On his back he wore a bundle that squeaked when he entered the clearing.

"Boys," said Zara. "These are friends from the future. They have come on a quest."

All at once, Julie realized that Urik's bundle was none other than his baby brother, Sparr.

The older boy bowed. "Urik, at your service. Mother, I just saw a shape without a shadow, a presence in our sacred woods."

The two children looked at each other.

"Holy cow! Are we dense?" said Julie.

"I know!" said Neal. "Wait a minute. About what?"

"It all makes sense now," said Julie. "It's so simple. That's how Ko finds out about you!"

"Something is simple?" said Neal.

"Wait," said Urik. "Who is Ko?"

"Ko is the terrible emperor of the beasts," said Julie. "He comes here from the world of Droon to . . . find you. But how does he know about you? It's so simple. He sends his creepy phantom here first. That's who is in your forest. Saba. He's Ko's phantom and a very bad creature."

Galen's jaw dropped. "Uh . . . that's a lot of information."

"It gets worse!" said Julie. "First of all —"

Suddenly, she paused. Was it right to tell them what would happen? Back in the present, Galen had warned them over and over not to share their knowledge of what would happen in the future. It could change the past and, therefore, change the present in ways they couldn't predict.

"Well, it just gets worse," she said.

"Then we need to defend the forest," said Zara. "Urik. If you don't mind?"

Her oldest son smiled slyly. "Oooh, I love this one. It's something new I thought up. Ready? Watch this!"

Urik waved his arms and hummed a little tune under his breath. All at once, the trees began to grow together to form a wall. Leaves fluttered, branches slithered together, roots squeaked. In no time, a wall several feet thick had grown around them. As the children watched, it seemed to them that the whole wall moved and breathed as if it were alive.

Then Zara cocked her head and listened. "I hear this phantom creature coming. Galen, take Sparr to the tree house. Urik, children, hide in the trees. Hurry!"

Suddenly, a tremendous wind roared around the grove. The trees shook, the ground quaked, and the air darkened with the smell of smoke.

# Three

## To the Blue Flame

After an hour spent tramping across the rocky black earth, Eric and Keeah paused to catch their breath. They had scanned the skies every few minutes but had not seen Gethwing since they started out.

"He's still out there," Keeah murmured softly. "Not close, but not far, either. Don't ask me why he doesn't just show himself and attack."

Eric had wondered the same thing. Only one reason came to mind. "Maybe he needs us," he said.

"Needs us? But why? What for?"

"To help him find something," said Eric. "What if he was looking around, then saw us, but doesn't want to chase us anywhere? He wants to follow us."

Keeah looked at the distant mountains. To her, they seemed as black as the rest of the landscape. "Because he can't find it himself. Maybe he can't see the blue flame, either."

"Exactly," Eric said. "So if he is out there watching us, we need to try to throw him off the trail."

Keeah smiled. "Good idea. Sneaky?"

"Sneaky," Eric agreed.

The two friends zigzagged quickly across the plains, sometimes splitting up, sometimes turning back, often going far out of their way, all to confuse the moon dragon.

By the time they reached the base of the black mountains, Eric had noticed something else that bothered him. They had been in this strange place for hours, but the light hadn't changed at all. Besides that, there was no wind. No breeze. No natural sounds. The more he thought about it, the more it seemed as if he and Keeah were not *outside* at all.

Instead, when Eric glanced up, the sky seemed to him like the underside of a vast black dome. What looked like a single star hung just above the mountaintop, exactly over the tiny blue flame.

"Ready to climb?" Keeah asked him.

"Ready," he said.

The rocks were sharp, and the way was

dangerously steep. Keeah went first, always keeping her eyes focused ahead, trying to find the safest route. Twice they had to backtrack because there was no way forward.

After several hours they were finally in sight of the top. But no sooner had they reached a narrow ledge below the summit than they heard the sound of rapidly padding feet above them and the same howl as before.

*Ah-roo* . . . .

"Something's up there," whispered Keeah. "I bet it doesn't want us to get any closer."

A second later, another howl overlapped the first. *Ah-rooo . . . ooo . . . ooo!*

"There are two of them," said Eric.

Keeah gulped. "It's too late to go back down. We have to go forward."

Eric nodded, and together they made their last and most difficult climb to the peak.

Only when they groped their way over the last shelf of rock did they realize that what Eric had thought was a cave was really a series of tall stones set side by side in a near-perfect circle.

"This is no natural rock formation," whispered Keeah. "Someone made this."

Two of the great stones were bent toward each other, forming an arched doorway into the circle. Between the stones, the children could see blue-tipped flames flickering inside a fire pit within.

Taking a breath to gather his courage, Eric nodded. "Okay, I'm going in."

"I'm right with you," said Keeah.

"Here I go."

"With me on your heels," said Keeah.

"I'm stepping inside right now."

"I'll cover you," said Keeah.

Eric stared into the ring of stones.

"Why aren't you moving?" asked Keeah.

"I thought I was," said Eric.

"No, you weren't."

Eric searched his mind. Something was preventing him from entering the stone circle, but it wasn't fear. He didn't feel afraid.

No, it was something else.

The place was solemn and silent. The fire leaped and danced, but made no sound. Eric felt as if he were standing in front of . . . as if it were . . . as if . . .

"It's like a holy place," Keeah whispered.

"You feel it, too!" said Eric. "A holy place. In the middle of all this . . . nothing."

He gazed back at the dark plains. Something moved swiftly across the earth, zigzagging here and there in the same pattern they had run. He knew instantly that it was Gethwing. The moon dragon was following their trail to the mountains.

"He tracked us," said Eric. "I'm going in!"

"After me!" said Keeah.

The two friends dashed under the rocky archway. When they did, the blue flames flared brightly, and while they gave off no smoke, the air was filled with the scent of something sweet.

*Apples?* thought Eric. *It smells like apples.*

"What is this place?" asked Keeah. "Or should I ask, *whose* place is this?"

Spanning the fire pit like a sort of

bridge was a thick stone that gleamed like iron and was itself blue when licked by the flames.

Tools, hammers, tongs, rods, mangled chunks of iron, and bars of silver were strewn across the ground around the fire pit.

"It's a forge," said Eric, stepping toward it. "A workshop. Someone is making something." Even as he spoke the words, Eric's chest began to heave. *Making something?*

Who was supposed to be *making something?*

It couldn't be. Could it?

But things that couldn't be seemed to be happening all around him.

"It looks like jewelry," said Keeah, pointing to several small amulets in the ashes.

Eric took up one amulet. Etched on its

face was a design he had seen before — an upside-down triangle with a lightning bolt through the center of it. His heart began to pound against his ribs. "Keeah . . ."

It had suddenly come to him where they might be. "We can't actually be . . . there. . . ."

Keeah turned to him. "I don't like the sound of that. We can't be where?"

"I think we might be in . . . the Underworld. Droon's Underworld," said Eric.

Keeah turned to him. "The Underworld? Why did Salamandra send us here? There's nothing in the Underworld. It's barren. No one lives here except . . . uhhhh!" She gasped.

Eric knew it, too. He could still barely believe what he was thinking, yet he couldn't help speaking the name.

"Sparr —"

Keeah shook her head. "This can't be his forge, can it? Oh, my gosh! This *is* his forge! Salamandra said, 'Put it all together.' What if she meant the Moon Medallion? There are four pieces to the Medallion. Zara created the base, but her sons were supposed to make the other parts. What if we're in the future at the exact moment when Sparr makes his piece? What if Salamandra sent us here to find it?! Eric —"

There was a movement in the back of the cave, and the two children dived into the shadows. Eric felt his limbs go weak as he watched a two-headed dog hobble out from behind the rocks.

It was Kem, Sparr's aged pet.

The old dog paused at the fire, sniffed at it, turned one gray head back toward the rocks, then turned the other.

"Is there anyone?" said a voice. "No?"

Eric's blood turned to ice. Keeah trembled next to him. The last time they had seen Sparr, he was leaping into a bottomless pit with Kem. Though many thought he had died, Eric had never stopped hoping he'd see Sparr again.

A crunch of gravel, a groan, and there was Lord Sparr. He moved slowly among the rocks toward the fire. He was old, very old, and thin and frail. His terrible sorcerer fins, once jagged reminders of his beastly past, had completely disappeared.

His spiked helmet was off. His hair, always jet-black, was now completely silver. His beard — also silver — hung nearly as long as his brother Galen's.

"Oh, my gosh, what's happened to him?" Keeah whispered. "Kem is old, too. How far into the future are we?"

Eric knew Sparr was a sorcerer and a

son of Zara. He wouldn't age as quickly as a normal man. But looking like this? How many years had passed since they left Droon?

Sparr stopped before the fire as if hypnotized by it. He stood there for a long time, saying nothing. When sound came from him, Eric did not see the sorcerer's lips move.

Sparr said a single word.

"Mother . . ."

All at once, Eric saw a face rise from the fire. It was a woman. Her skin was as white as snow. Her hair was black. Her image seemed as alive as the fire itself.

Eric's chest ached. His head throbbed.

"Zara?" he whispered.

"What?" asked Keeah, peering over his shoulder. "Where's Zara? You see Zara?"

Like a glimmering shadow, the shape of the queen emerged from the tongues of flame. She rose above the fire, then moved to her son's side and whispered into his ear. She took his hands as he worked the hammer and tongs, gesturing, speaking in musical tones.

"She's talking to him!" Eric whispered.

Keeah moved aside to try to get a better look.

Along with his other powers, Eric had lost his ability to know what Zara was saying to Sparr. But from the way the sorcerer changed his tools or drove the tongs into the fire, he knew she was instructing him.

Sparr drew a red-hot object from the flames and set it on the stone. Then he took up a long, sharpened tool and began to scratch the surface of the device.

Eric couldn't believe what he saw next.

While normally a thing drawn from a fire cools, the object Sparr had made did not. With each letter the sorcerer engraved upon it, the device grew brighter, and the ring of stones hummed as if they were giant chimes.

But there was another sound, too, faint at first, then louder, and the image of the queen vanished. When Eric turned to the open arch behind him, he heard it more clearly.

*Whooo-ooo!* The sound was closing in.

Eric stood, his hands tightening into fists.

"Gethwing!" he said. "No way —"

"Who's there?" said Sparr, his voice faint.

"Gethwing's coming, Sparr," said Keeah, bouncing out from her hiding place.

"Gethwing," said the sorcerer, as if still entranced. "I've heard that name before."

"You can't let him take what you've

made," said Eric. "It's why he's come. You need that device. Droon needs it!"

Sparr jerked his head. His eyelids flicked open and closed several times, as if he just now recognized the children. "Gethwing? Coming for this? No, no. I've been working too many years."

"Years?" repeated Eric. "Sparr, we've come from the past. How long have you been here?"

Sparr's eyes focused on a nearby stone that was scratched with marks from top to bottom. "The number stands at a round fifty years."

"Fifty years!" said Eric. "Whoa —"

Gethwing broke the air with a howl.

"The dragon comes!" said Sparr, tearing himself away from the fire. "Stand fast, children. Kem, behind me. Eric, with me now. You are needed. Keeah, you as well. The three of us together!"

"But I lost my powers," said Eric. "Besides, we're sort of defenseless up here."

"Oh?" A thin smile curled over Sparr's lips, reminding Eric of the powerful sorcerer he used to know. "Before I understood what I was to make, I forged these. Kem?"

The old dog pounced on a pile of rocks and ashes and discarded metal objects. From it, he pulled three long blades. They were crooked, misshapen, wicked-looking swords with edges as jagged as saws.

"Battle blades!" said Keeah.

Sparr grinned. "I had to test the fire somehow, didn't I?"

One blade coiled, another was curved like a ship's keel, while the third zig-zagged like a lightning bolt.

"Now these swords shall be tested in a real battle," said Sparr. "And I think we shall be tested, too, no?"

"Yes," said Keeah, cutting the air with her sword.

"Come, Eric," said Sparr, taking up position on the summit. "Real power is in the heart. You may have no magic, but is your heart strong?"

"I think so," said Eric.

"Yes?" asked Sparr, searching him with his black eyes.

"Yes," said Eric. "Yes!"

"Then fight for your life!" said Sparr.

No sooner had he spoken than the terrifying black wings of the moon dragon flashed overhead, and Gethwing dived at the ring of stones.

# Four

## The Moon and the Smoke

Neal's fingers sparked inside the fortress of trees. Julie stood behind Zara and Urik. Galen, just back from hiding baby Sparr, crouched next to them, poised for Saba's attack.

As solid a wall as the trees made, the phantom battered them. He tore at them with his four powerful hands. Again and again he charged at the trees. All at once, there was a squeal of pain and a tree flew out of the earth and hurtled across the grove.

"Tree killer!" said Galen. "I don't like you!"

Saba charged into the grove howling. "Arrr! I have hunted you for days. Now I find you! My master, Ko, wants magic! He shall have yours!"

"How about . . . no!" yelled Urik.

With all their might, the three wizards stood together like a wall. They raised their fingers and fired at Saba.

*Wha—boooom!*

With a blast that shook the forest, the phantom was hurled out of the grove and vanished away into the trees.

The grove was suddenly quiet.

"He will return," said Zara.

"He's like a robot," said Neal. "With

only one thing on his mind, if you can call it that."

"Neal, Julie," said Zara. "Quickly tell us what you know about Ko and Saba. Do not spare us!"

The two children looked at each other.

Julie began. "Back in our time, Emperor Ko is leader of the Dark Lands. He's able to send his creepy phantom, Saba, through time to get things he wants."

"And he wants lots of stuff," said Neal.

"Right now, in our time, Ko is attacking the capital of Droon, trying to burn it down. It's a beautiful place called Jaffa City," said Julie. She turned to Galen. "You live there now."

"Me?" said Galen.

Urik nudged his brother. "Sounds like the *Galen Chronicles* will go to several volumes!"

Zara closed her eyes and opened them again. "Droon is a name that has played about my mind recently. Perhaps I go to Droon in the future."

"You do," said Neal. He paused, wondering what he could say about the future. "I mean . . . maybe you do . . ."

"Perhaps we meet again in your time," said Zara.

Neither child could find a way to tell the queen exactly what would happen. How after Ko kidnapped Zara and her infant son, his curse left Sparr an orphan.

"Your silence speaks volumes. I understand," said Zara. She paced the grove, then stopped at the great white stone. "Our two worlds are filled with dangers. I have long pondered creating something to contain my magic for when I am no longer here. To bind the forces of our family together, no matter what happens. You could use it to stop Ko in the future." The queen turned to the children. "I will make it now."

The next hour seemed to go by in seconds. While Galen and Urik repaired the wall of trees and scanned the edges of the grove with sparking fingers, Neal and Julie watched as Zara created a disk of brilliant white silver on the magic forge.

As the moon's light shone down, illuminating her every move, Zara painstakingly etched the disk with symbols that seemed to come alive as soon as she finished them. Letters, words, characters — all swam across its silvery surface, humming, whispering, singing of unimaginable magic and power.

Neal and Julie were entranced.

Soon, the queen lifted her head.

"The Moon Medallion is finished," she said. "Its true power can only be revealed to my sons and their sons and their sons. Let's hope it never falls into the wrong hands."

It came to Julie then with the force of a tidal wave. She pulled Neal aside. "Oh, my gosh! This is why we're here! Salamandra said to put it all together. The Moon Medallion is made of four parts. But maybe Zara doesn't know that yet. We have to collect the parts. Salamandra said it will save Droon!"

Neal's eyes bugged out. "Zara has to know, but we can't exactly tell her. It has to be her idea. Also, Galen and Urik don't know they're supposed to make them, right?"

"Right," said Julie. "We have to tell her secretly. And cleverly."

Neal grinned. "Leave it to me!"

While Urik and Galen patrolled the

grove around them, the children went to the queen.

"Uh, you know, that Medallion is great," said Neal. "All silver and stuff. But wouldn't it be even better with some, you know, attachments on it?"

"Attachments?" asked Zara.

"Parts," said Julie. "Like a part from Galen, and one from Urik. That kind of thing."

They looked at the queen.

"I like it the way it is," she said.

Neal grumbled. "Okay, clever didn't work. Queen Zara, with all due respect, there are actually four parts to the Moon Medallion."

Zara frowned. "Four parts?"

"Neal's right," said Julie. "What you've just made is the first part. Galen and Urik will make their own parts, only they won't know it until the time is right. Even baby Sparr will one day make something. Only when the pieces are united does the Medallion reveal its true power."

Zara's face beamed with silver light as she held the Medallion in her hands. "To bring my sons together when they are needed! To unite them and their magic, no matter where or when they are. Yes, what a great idea!"

"And, PS?" said Neal. "It's *your* idea."

All at once, the walls of the grove quaked.

A sudden wind swept around the trees.

"He's back!" yelled Galen, bounding back to his mother and the children.

Saba burst violently into the grove, sending trees flying in every direction. It was clear that he sensed great magic. With a speed that startled everyone, the phantom flew at Zara, knocking her down. The

Moon Medallion fell from her hands and rolled across the ground.

"Oh, no you don't!" shouted Urik. He dived and snatched up the disk. "That's ours!"

"This is yours, too!" Saba boomed. "I searched and searched and discovered its hiding place."

He pulled something out from behind his back. It was a tiny bundle. It squeaked.

"Sparr!" Zara screamed. "You wicked beast! Give me my son!"

"Give me your magic!" shouted Saba.

"You want it?" said the queen. "Jump for it!" She threw the Medallion up into the air, and the grove exploded in silver light.

Neal shielded his eyes, but between his fingers he glimpsed amazing things.

Shapes flew out of the Medallion like

fleeing ghosts. A shape like the Ring of Midnight flew around and around until it struck Galen and vanished. The Pearl Sea did the same over Urik's head. Something that looked like a many-pointed star, beaming and glowing from its blades, shot up in the air and fell on the bundle that Saba held in his hands.

"Ko wants your magic!" boomed Saba. He threw the bundle high, and a soaring snake swooped through the trees, grabbing it and flying away with it.

"A wingsnake!" cried Julie.

"Sparr! No!" cried Galen.

Saba wrenched the Medallion from the air. The moment his claws wrapped around it — *boom!* — the grove exploded in smoke, and Saba vanished, leaving a weaving trail of smoke behind him.

"Where is he?" said Zara.

"Gone into his own stinky smoke!" said Urik.

Galen flicked his fingers, and the flames subsided. Zara jumped up, clutching her arm.

"You're hurt," said Julie.

"Not enough to stop me!" said the queen. "Galen, you and I will find Sparr. Urik, go with the children. Save the Medallion. Julie, Neal, if you find it, take it back to Droon with you. You need it now. Return it when you can. Go!"

As quickly as they could, the queen and her son raced after the wingsnake that had kidnapped Sparr, while Urik, Neal, and Julie dashed away through the forest after the phantom thief.

# Five

# Burned by Silver Fire

The shadows of four black wings fell over Eric, Keeah, and Sparr as the moon dragon bounded into the ring of stones.

"Gethwing!" said Sparr. "You vile thing! Children, now!"

While the sorcerer charged with his sword raised high, Keeah blasted purple sparks at the dragon's wings, and Eric ran at his chest with his own jagged blade. Their assault was strong, but it was Kem's two sets of teeth nipping at the dragon's feet that sent the beast fleeing back up into the air.

"Good work!" said Sparr with a laugh. "The first round goes to us! He'll return. Luckily, this ring of stones is like a hand. A hand that can become a fist. Watch closely!"

With a nod, he spoke words to the stone. *"Prostoh-selat-nefna-zarak!"*

Obeying his command, the stone walls rang with music and grew together into a formidable fortress of stone with a dome for a lid.

"Amazing!" said Keeah.

"A trick I learned long ago," said Sparr. "The better to protect my creation."

Eric turned to the anvil. He couldn't take his eyes off of the gleaming object that sat there. It was a small, star-shaped object made of silver.

"What is it?" he asked.

"I call it the Twilight Star," said the sorcerer. "An image lived indistinct in my mind for many years. Only lately have I seen it clearly enough to forge it."

Sparr gazed at the Twilight Star, spoke a soft word, and immediately the object lifted into the air and began to spin.

As it spun, the Star sometimes seemed to have three points, sometimes thirty. Sometimes it paused in its own radiant glow, while at other times it spun so swiftly that it beamed like a solid disk of silver light.

As Eric beheld the Star, his mind whirled. Since he had first realized that he and Keeah were in the Underworld, he had wondered if Neal and Julie were together, too.

He had wondered if, in fact, his friends had gone into the past seeking the base of the Moon Medallion and Urik's Pearl Sea.

Then he no longer wondered if they were.

He knew they were.

"She came to you," said Eric. "Zara came to you. She guided your work."

Sparr looked at Eric for a long moment, then turned to the fire. "I know my brothers each made parts of the Medallion. These parts have been safe at Jaffa City these fifty long years. Now my Star can be added to them to create the greatest magic known to either world."

The children shared a look.

"You don't know, then," said Eric.

Sparr turned back. "Know what?"

"Ko attacked Jaffa City," said Keeah. "Fifty years ago. Back in our present. We weren't there to help Galen and my parents."

"We fear the worst," said Eric.

Sparr's eyes flashed, and he ran his

fingers behind his ears where his batlike fins used to be. "Then you must return to your present, return to Jaffa City. You must take my Star —"

With no warning, the dome of rock quaked with a thunderous explosion, and suddenly Gethwing stood among them, laughing.

"And now — you perish!" cried the dragon. "Princess, I will take you first. And throw in the powerless little boy for free!"

Gethwing charged at Keeah and Eric with arms extended.

"Not so!" Sparr yelled. As old as he was, he flew between the children and the dragon, hacking with his sword while blasting repeatedly with beams of red sparks.

Gethwing tried to press forward, but Sparr drove him back outside the broken ring.

Wailing, the dragon once more took to the skies and circled high overhead.

Eric got to his feet and helped Keeah up. "You saved us!"

The sorcerer smiled. "Many is the time I would not have, Eric Hinkle." He snatched the Twilight Star from the fire pit. It blossomed with silver light in his hand.

The moon dragon dived once more into the ring. His eyes flamed with desire and rage.

"From the moment Salamandra betrayed me and sent me here, something drew me," he snarled. "I knew not what it was, until I saw the children seeking this place. Long ago, I tried to steal the Pearl Sea. You defeated me then. Let me now return the favor. If I am to rule over Ko, over Droon, I need this magic. Give me the Star!"

With a suddenness that made Eric reel, Gethwing leaped across the fire and flung out his massive arm at Sparr, throwing him to the edge of the peak. Sparr teetered on the edge for a moment, then fell to the ground like a dead weight.

Then, with blow after blow, the moon dragon tore down the fortress of stones, toppling the giant rocks one after another.

Kem leaped over to Sparr, but in the quickness of Gethwing's attack he could do nothing. The massive stones collapsed on both the dog and his master.

"No!" cried Eric.

Only Sparr's hand was visible. In it he held the silver Star.

"So easy to take," said Gethwing, eyeing the Star. "But first a little housekeeping. Eliminate the princess!" With a sudden, powerful blast, the dragon threw her outside the ring of fallen stones.

Eric ran to help Keeah, but the moon dragon stepped in his way. "I have spared you often, boy," he sneered. "Those days are at an end. Within my grasp is the power I have sought for ages. After all these years, these *very* long years, Gethwing will triumph!"

With that, Gethwing knocked Eric to the ground. He landed hard, striking his head on the ground.

"And now, with no wizards left to stop me, I finish the job!" snarled the dragon. He marched, step-by-step, toward Sparr.

Eric climbed to his feet. It angered him to see Gethwing approach the fallen sorcerer so proudly.

After all, Sparr was a son of Zara.

Sparr was a brother of Galen and Urik.

His life could not end this way!

"No . . . you . . . don't," said Eric. In one swift move, he dived at Sparr and pulled the Twilight Star from his hand.

He expected the Star to burn him, and it did. But not with heat. The silver Star was icier than he could have imagined.

Its freezing touch burned his fingers.

But he gripped it tight and whirled around to face the moon dragon. Even as he did, however, Gethwing's powerful claws ripped the Star from him and hurled him across the peak. The moon dragon turned once more toward Sparr.

The look in Gethwing's eyes had always frightened Eric, but there was little more for him to fear now.

If his powers were gone, then fine. He would perish right then and there, doing what he knew was right.

It was in that hopelessness, in that despair, that he found himself moving

toward the moon dragon, his fists hard-
ening.

"You — will — not — win!" he cried.

And with that, Eric grabbed Sparr's
sword from the rubble and ran at
Gethwing.

## Six

# Hand to Hand

With Sparr's sword held high, Eric charged at the moon dragon, hacking at his wings, but Gethwing leaped away onto a pile of stony rubble.

"You have annoyed me for the last time!"

"Oh, really?" said Eric, raising the sword again. "Because I think I could go on like this for years!"

The dragon's face darkened with

rage. His black wings filled the sky overhead.

"Fight me!" cried Eric fiercely.

Gethwing pounced at him. Eric fought the dragon — powerlessly, valiantly — raining blow after blow on the beast's black scales. One after another he blocked the dragon's swiping assaults with Sparr's sword. He fought and he fought. And in his pain, he fought some more.

Finally, the moon dragon flew up to the topmost of the collapsed stones.

"Afraid?" said Eric, his chest heaving.

Saying nothing, Gethwing raised a terrible clawed hand. An instant later — *whoomf!* — his hand glowed in flames.

The flames grew to monstrous size until they formed a ball of raging fire.

Gethwing's massive leathery tail coiled and hissed through the air like an angry snake.

"Eric Hinkle!" he boomed. "This is your last moment. Prepare to —"

"You shall never!" cried a voice from the ashes.

Gethwing turned as Sparr leaped up, fingers sizzling with sparks, and flew at him.

Eric felt a hand throw him clear across the mountaintop into Keeah just as the fireball exploded.

The mountain peak quaked.

Eric thought he saw the fireball strike Sparr in the head. Then Gethwing lunged at the sorcerer, howling at the top of his lungs.

"This — is — the — end!"

"No . . . no!" shouted Eric. With his last ounce of strength, he dived across the peak at Gethwing. At the same time, Keeah leaped after Eric. They tumbled together to the edge.

"Take my hand!" she cried.

Eric took her hand and held tight.

When he looked down, he saw the great, dark-winged shape of Gethwing plummeting off the summit into the abyss below.

Clutching him in furious battle was Lord Sparr, finless, helmetless, silver-haired, his eyes filled with fire and courage, his sparking fists hammering the dragon's chest. Kem was there, too, biting both of Gethwing's ears from behind.

The moon dragon howled and howled.

Together, Eric and Keeah watched Gethwing and Sparr and Kem fall, fall, fall off the mountaintop, thudding from ledge to ledge, head over heels, striking one jagged stone after another, crying out until all that remained were the echoes.

The two friends stared down into the darkness until they could see no more.

"Oh, my gosh!" whispered Keeah. "What happened here? Did Sparr... is he...?"

Eric's throat tightened. His chest heaved. He couldn't believe what his eyes saw. Sparr was gone...lost....Sparr was...dead?

And then it came.

No more than a tiny speck of light at first, an object came spinning up from the depths toward the two friends.

Reaching his hands out, Eric leaped up and caught it.

It was the Twilight Star.

"The final piece of the Medallion," said Keeah. "It's what we need to save Droon!"

"Sparr gave it to us," said Eric.

"To you," said Keeah.

"To Droon."

The Star's silver light seemed to beam

straight up at the single light in the Underworld's sky.

"And that's just where we have to go," said Keeah. "To Droon. To Jaffa City."

Eric looked up, too. "That's the hole Sparr jumped through to get to the Underworld. It's how we'll get back up to Droon."

Keeah tried to smile. "Some quests never end."

For the next hour, the two friends climbed silently and quickly. From rock to rock, they scaled the tallest and blackest peak of the tall, black mountain, but their thoughts were far below in the abyss with Sparr.

Keeah couldn't believe she had seen the sorcerer plunge to his death. Eric kept thinking of how, even in death, Sparr had given him an object of wondrous power.

Finally, they reached the mountain's

summit and stood directly below the opening between the Underworld and the world of Droon.

Keeah turned to Eric. "It's not far. I'm pretty sure I can fly us up there."

"But what will we find?" he asked.

"I'm afraid to think," she said. "Fifty years is a long time."

"I have a feeling it's going to be bad," said Eric. "Very bad."

The princess nodded silently. She was thinking of her parents. Of Galen. Of Max. Even of her future self. What would she find?

Eric wondered the same thing. Did Ko win his battle against the forces of good? If he did, Droon would be frightening. Unimaginable.

He looked at the Star in his hand, then stuffed it into his pocket. He hoped he was up for the journey.

"It's time," said Keeah. She put her hand in his. "Ready?"

"What if I said no?"

She smiled. "I'd say . . . that makes two of us. But we have to go anyway."

"Then let's do it."

With a quick crouch and a jump, the two friends leaped straight up through the ceiling of the Underworld's black dome and toward the Droon of the future.

# Seven

## Palace of Smoke

It took Urik, Julie, and Neal little time to follow Saba's smoky trail through Zara's enchanted forest.

Beyond the edge of the trees lay a round lake of twinkling blue water.

But when Urik looked closely, he stopped dead. On an island in the center of the lake stood a vast, purple-walled palace.

"I never saw that before!" said Urik. "I mean, that place doesn't even exist!"

"I bet it's something like a phantom palace," said Neal. "It probably travels between this world and Droon."

Julie and Urik shared a look.

"You think?" asked Urik.

"Not often, but I keep trying," said Neal. "For instance, let's say that maybe Saba can vanish because he's really just a phantom. But the Medallion is a solid object. It needs an opening to get from here to Droon."

Julie turned to Neal. "Did you think of that all by yourself?"

Neal grinned. "It must be the turban. I'm not usually this smart. Plus, look at the symbol on the palace gates," he added, pointing to a triangle with horns carved into the purple doors. "That's totally Ko's sign. It's like he can't have anything that doesn't have his name on it."

Urik scanned the high purple walls. "Well, I think sometimes, too. And I think I'm glad to have you two on this quest!"

"Let's get in there," said Julie. "Before Saba takes off to Droon and it's too late."

With a single fluid move, Urik swept his hands over the lake, and it froze, allowing the three friends to cross to the city quickly.

As they hurried across the frozen water, the moon began to set, and the sky turned black.

Once they were on the island, Urik moved his hands over the purple gates. The doors creaked once, twice, then popped open. Inside, the entryway was dark.

Urik peered into the gloom. "Looks like a maze inside."

"Saba has given us a puzzle," said Neal.

"Add it to the list," said Julie. She turned to Urik. "I hope we know what we're doing."

The wizard smiled. "Me, too. Me, too."

Neal and Julie followed Urik into the palace of purple stones. Its passages were narrow and winding. The air was as purple as the stone, and it smelled thickly of smoke.

"What a place," said Neal, waving the heavy air from his face. "Of course, it's just the sort of place Saba would go for. Smelly."

The floor beneath them rumbled suddenly.

"That probably isn't anything good," said Julie. "We'd better find the Medallion before this place vanishes — and we vanish with it."

As the little group dashed from hallway to passage to tunnel, they saw no one, yet felt that eyes were on them every moment.

Soon they arrived in the palace's central courtyard. From there, they could see what looked like the main palace hall.

Urik turned. "It could be dangerous in there. Everyone up for it?"

"It's why I'm here," said Julie.

"Ditto," added Neal.

Together the friends made their way into a tall, columned room whose walls of white stone glowed with light from torch flames.

The center of the room contained not a throne, as they expected, but a pool ten feet from its outer rim to its center. It was filled with something that bubbled, but wasn't water.

"What is that?" said Urik, waving the air in front of his face.

The pool was brimming with smoke. It

drifted and moved about, coiling and furling from somewhere far below.

"That's Saba's way to Droon," said Julie. "That's how he'll take the Medallion to Ko."

Holding his nose and peering in, Neal saw that there was no bottom to the pool, and though the smoke was very dark, he could see the skies of none other than Droon's Dark Lands below.

"So I was actually right?" he whispered. "This pool does lead right to Ko's hideout? We can't let Saba take the Medallion down there."

All at once, there came a sound like the rushing of wind through the palace hallways.

"Saba," hissed Neal.

"Hide!" said Urik.

The three friends slid into the shadows of the room. When Saba strode in, his

frightening face glowed silver from the Medallion in his hands.

The phantom stood at the edge of the smoky pool. He raised the Medallion over the pool. Then he began to chant. The children recognized the words as being from Goll, the ancient kingdom of Emperor Ko.

All at once, Saba's chanting ceased, and the smoke began to whirl around in the pool as if stirred quickly by a giant, invisible spoon.

The same thing happened to the room itself.

"The palace — the whole city — is starting to vanish!" hissed Julie.

Saba howled once, then stepped onto the rim of the pool. He closed his three eyes.

"Now!" cried Urik. The three friends burst out from the shadows. Julie shot like an arrow at Saba, pushing him off the pool's rim. Urik lunged for the Medallion and snatched it away from Saba.

Already the phantom had begun to dissolve into the smoke of the pool.

"Oh, too bad!" said Neal. "Can't stop your own spell, can you? That's a shame."

But the phantom's chant had another effect, too. While it made Saba turn to smoke, the smoke coiling up from the pool assumed another shape. Many other shapes.

And the room filled with a swarm of snarling wingsnakes.

"Holy cow!" cried Julie. "Ko sent his friends! He really wants this Medallion!"

*Sssss!* the wingsnakes hissed angrily.

"I guess that's our cue to bolt!" said Urik.

"I'm already gone!" said Neal.

# Eight

# And . . . They're Off!

Julie, Neal, and Urik raced through the halls of the dissolving palace with a pack of snarling wingsnakes on their heels. The three friends dashed out the gates.

Neal looked up at the sky. It was dark and getting darker quickly. Wind whirled over Zara's forest.

"My genie sense tells me that the Portal is only a few minutes away," he said. "We'd better hurry or we'll miss it!"

No sooner had they charged back across the ice bridge than the palace dissolved and the island vanished.

"We did it!" said Julie.

"Uh, not quite," said Urik. "Those wingsnakes don't know that they're not supposed to be here!"

"Run!" said Neal. "And keep running!"

They ran all the way back to the forest.

The storm of wind was getting closer every moment. Julie and Neal sped ahead, trying to get under it, when they noticed that Urik had stopped.

"What is it?" Julie asked. "We have to hurry to the safety of your mother's grove."

Urik shook his head. "I see it."

"You see what?" asked Neal.

"A part of the Medallion," said Urik. "I think . . . I think I need to make it. I need to make my piece of the Medallion."

Neal felt his heart skip a beat. "Now?"

"Right now," said Urik. "I need to make it to keep the Medallion's magic powerful."

Neal looked behind them. "The wing-snakes are coming. Can you make it while you run really, really fast? Those wing-snakes' eyes see everything. Especially food. And I think they think we're food!"

"Food?" said Urik. He smiled suddenly. "Neal, thanks for the idea —"

"Oh, not you, too!" cried Julie. "The snakes!"

Still smiling, Urik pulled the two children through a thicket of vines and into a grove of apple trees. He looked up at the branches, which were heavy with red fruit.

"I've had a vision that hasn't been clear to me until this moment," he said. "Now it is."

He plucked an apple from a low branch and shined it on his sleeve.

"I love apples," he said.

"Me, too," said Neal. "Especially the pie kind. But the wingsnakes —"

"Neal, *shhh!*" said Julie, spellbound.

Urik moved the apple into a shaft of moonlight, and it began to change. In the bright glow of the moon, the apple turned from red to silver. Then Urik rolled the silver fruit over in his hands until it became a small, round stone.

It shone silvery white under the moon.

"It's a stone whose heart moves within it like the motion of waves," explained the young wizard. "It's sometimes cloudy, like our own lives. It's sometimes clear, like the ocean at night, all silver with moonlight. I think I will call it the Stone of Waves."

Neal frowned. "Or maybe the Pearl Sea."

Urik scratched his chin. "I don't know . . . maybe Ocean Ball? Or how about Water Globe? I like that —"

"Believe me," said Julie. "It's called the Pearl Sea!"

Urik laughed. "Well, it does have a certain ring to it. The Pearl Sea it is." He looked up at the silver moon above their heads. "Neal, Julie, my mother's Moon Medallion is very powerful. It contains all my mother's mystical knowledge. But now I know that its greatest power can only be released when all its parts are brought together."

"Like a family," said Julie.

Urik laughed. "Exactly. When it's all together, a word like 'magic' is too small to describe what the Medallion will be able to do."

The children tried to imagine what magic the Medallion held.

"Wow," said Neal.

The young wizard smiled. "You can say that again."

"Wow," Neal repeated

All at once, the wingsnakes spotted them and swarmed into the grove. There were hundreds of them now. They hissed and snarled and prepared to pounce.

"I think we've waited too long," said Urik.

The bushes rustled suddenly, and a boy in a blue tunic with a sparkling staff bounded in.

"Galen!" said Neal.

"We found Sparr safe and sound, shooting baby-blue sparks at the wingsnake. But I see that snake brought some brothers and sisters!"

Urik nodded. "Who don't like us much."

"The feeling is mutual," said Galen. "Wait a second. I think I'll have to add another chapter to the *Galen Chronicles*. I'll call this one 'The Defeat of the Flying Snakes.'"

"Cool," said Neal. "But let's be sure there's no sequel called 'The Revenge of the Flying Snakes'!"

Galen laughed. "I like how you think."

"I've been doing some thinking of my own," said Urik. "And I think it's time for you kids to enter that Portal. Take the Medallion and the Pearly Ocean with you —"

"The Pearl Sea," said Neal.

"That's the one," said Urik. "You need them more than we do right now."

"Until then, we fight!" said Galen.

"Rock on!" said Neal.

"Ditto!" added Julie.

Together the two wizard brothers waded into the swarm of hissing wing-snakes, blasting away and hacking with their blazing staffs.

Neal and Julie knew that the wizard family would stand side by side for only a little longer before they were broken up forever. It was amazing to see them together. But as the roar of battle grew louder, the Portal of Ages screamed and howled, too.

Hand in hand, Julie and Neal ran toward the spinning storm.

"Ayeeee!" Julie cried as the storm of wind sucked her in.

The second-to-last thought Neal had before everything turned black around him was of the magnificent Medallion and the shining pearl that Urik had fashioned out of next to nothing.

The last thought he had was of a bowl of macaroni and cheese.

"*Mmm,*" he murmured.

A moment later, he and Julie were lost in the Portal, hurtling through time.

# Nine

## The Dark Future

Eric and Keeah flew quickly from the Underworld to Droon while the Twilight Star's silvery beams guided their way.

The passage between the worlds coiled and zigzagged. Eric felt as if his mind was doing the same thing.

Was Sparr actually . . . gone?

How could he not perish in that fall?

Would they really never see him again?

"Keep reminding yourself," said Keeah as they flew higher, "it's a long time in the future now. There's no telling what we'll find."

Eric felt Keeah press his hand harder. "I think I'm ready."

"For anything?" she asked.

"Well, for some things."

But as ready as he was, Eric was not prepared for what they saw the moment they left the Underworld and flew out over Droon.

"Oh, no," said Keeah. "No . . . no."

As they swept up into the air, then drifted over the Droon Sea, they were stunned at what stood on the far coast.

It was Jaffa City.

Or what was left of it.

The tall pink towers and golden dome of the great royal capital of Droon were charred black, toppled, and fallen. The burning embers of great buildings smoldered in every quarter of the city. All around the crumbling walls were encampments of every type and description of beast.

Worst of all, a giant black flag emblazoned with Ko's terrifying symbol flew over the city's once-proud gates.

"Oh . . ." Keeah faltered. "Is this what happened after we entered the Portal fifty years ago? Did Ko win? Does Ko rule over all of Droon now?"

Eric didn't know what to say. What *could* he say? "We'd better find a place to land."

"Yes . . . yes . . ." she said.

Choking as much on her own tears as from the smoke, Keeah veered away from the city toward the only patch of green they could see.

Eric recognized it as the very northern edge of the Farne Woods. Much of the forest had been destroyed, cut down, or burned black.

"Down there," said Eric, pointing to the trees. "Smoke. White smoke. The good kind."

Through the thick canopy of branches, Keeah spied the source of the smoke.

It was a small, rustic cabin.

Her heart trembled as she recognized her birthplace, the king and queen's tiny cottage where they were first married.

Eric remembered it as the place where Keeah had found her long-lost magic harp.

"It's still standing," she said. "I wonder if my parents are there."

"At least some Ninns are," said Eric. Near the cottage sat a half dozen large, red-faced warriors around a campfire. "Let's land."

The two children circled the woods and touched down among the trees. The moment they approached the cabin, the startled Ninns glanced up, screamed, then fled into the woods, leaving their campfires sputtering.

"What's wrong?" asked Eric. "They look like they've seen a couple of ghosts."

Keeah gulped. "Maybe they have. This is a new, dark future, remember? Maybe we're much older now. Maybe we're even . . . even . . ."

"Don't say it!" said Eric, suddenly imagining a future without Keeah or him in it.

"Who's there?" said a voice.

The front door of the cottage creaked open. In the doorway stood an old man. His hair and beard were very long and as white as snow.

"Galen?" whispered Keeah, taking a step toward him. "Oh, no . . ."

It *was* Galen. The great wizard tottered on the steps and squinted at the two

children, his hands gripping his long, curved staff as if he needed it to stand.

When his dim eyes made them out, he yelped excitedly. "Keeah! Eric! Oh, my!"

He hobbled to them and hugged them with arms that were still strong. "You have no idea what it means to see you! I long suspected it would happen just this way!"

The children shared a look.

"What do you mean?" asked Keeah.

Galen smiled as he led them toward the cottage. "You see," he said, "no sooner had you children vanished into the Portal of Ages than you returned."

"We did?" said Eric.

"Yes, but it was already too late," said Galen. "Ko attacked Jaffa City, stole the Moon Medallion, and defeated us. Over the years — the many years! — we survivors have lived in the hope that this dark future did not have to happen. Now the fact that you have returned — young again — has given me hope and has frightened the poor Ninns. Captain Bludge! See who has come!"

When Lord Sparr's former warriors returned slowly and hesitantly from the woods, the children saw that their pointed ears drooped, their plump cheeks were sunken, and their battle swords — never far from their sides — were dented and battle-worn.

"For a long time we believed you might return as children. Then we stopped believing," said a large warrior. "Is it true, then, after all these years? Are you really . . . *you*?"

Eric remembered Bludge as the captain of a friendly group of Ninns they had met before. "We've come from fifty years in the past," he said.

"The Portal took us from the eve of the battle for Jaffa City to now," said Keeah.

"The war you saw begin has continued to this day," said Bludge, speaking in a manner neither child had ever heard before. "One by one, all the forces of good in Droon have fallen. Only we are left."

A faint cough came from behind Galen. He stood aside, and there stood Max, the spider troll. Keeah ran to him and hugged him.

Max's wild orange hair had turned nearly completely gray, and what remained was thin. His eyes were dim, but he smiled when he saw his old friends.

"Many things have happened in the time since we have seen you this way," he said. "Jaffa City is home to Ko now. No one has seen you children — *as* children — since the city fell so many years ago."

Max and Galen shared a quick look.

To Eric it seemed as if they knew something they did not want to tell. "Go on," he said.

Max wiped his moist cheeks. "After Salamandra sent you all into the Portal, my master, Galen, and I raced back on our flying carpet to stop Ko's attack."

"I remember," said Keeah. "It's the last thing we saw before the storm took us away."

"The battle was terrible. It was only the first of many," said Max. "When the great city finally fell, those who survived hid here in the forest."

"Alas, my charms have aged with me," said Galen. "I had thought to retrieve my mother's Moon Medallion from my tower. I sought to use its power to battle Ko, but I failed. We cannot resist his armies any longer. Our battle, my friends, is over, and we have lost."

Keeah grew suddenly alarmed. "Where are my mother and father?"

Galen took a deep breath and looked back through the trees toward the city. "The first battle lasted seven years. The king and queen did not live to fight the second battle, nor the eighth, nor the tenth."

Keeah buried her face in her hands and sank to the ground. Max hobbled to her and wrapped his thin arms around her.

"Ah, child," said Galen, placing his hand on her shoulder. "My child . . . my dear . . ."

Eric's heart heaved into his throat. His legs trembled. Keeah's parents! Queen Relna and King Zello! Gone. Gone! He had often thought of them as his Droon parents. Of course it was the future, and time had passed, but still. How did it happen? Why did it happen?

Keeah wept and wept, and as she wept, Eric felt his mind begin to race until one thought came to him and refused to budge. Galen was right. A single hope remained. The only way to save Jaffa City from Ko's devastating attack was to make certain that the attack never took place. This wasn't how the future should turn out. It shouldn't be this way. And if he had anything to say about it, it *wouldn't* be this way.

"Galen, what can we do?" he asked. "Keeah and I believe that Salamandra sent us on a quest into the future for a reason. I think she wanted us to stop this. She must have thought it was possible. We'll do anything. *I'll* do anything."

Everyone turned to Galen. He was quiet for a long moment, then he spoke. "The truth is that only great magic can fight Ko now. But the Pearl Sea is no more. The base of the Medallion my mother made so long ago has also been destroyed. Only the Ring of Midnight remains intact. But once that is gone, Droon, all of it, will fall. The Empire of Goll will have returned."

Eric thrust his hand in his pocket and took out the Twilight Star. "We found Sparr's forge in the Underworld. We have his part of the Medallion."

Galen trembled to gaze upon the gleaming object. Then he turned to the Ninns. "Could this be the hope we have waited for?"

There came the sudden sound of a harp being plucked inside the cabin. This was followed by the squeak of a wheel spinning rapidly.

"What's that?" asked Keeah, climbing to her feet. "What's that noise?"

"See for yourself," said Galen, waving his hand toward the cottage door. "Behold the Queen of Droon."

"The queen? But you said —" Keeah

rushed through the cottage door and saw her magic harp, floating in the center of the room, playing a soft melody. On a little stool behind the harp sat a young woman bent over a stone wheel that she turned with foot pedals. Against the swiftly turning wheel, she held a silver sword.

"Queen?" said Keeah.

The woman turned her face up from the wheel.

Keeah gasped. The woman was her older self, beautiful, grown up, but still young.

"Oh!" said the queen. She leaped up from the stool and grasped her younger self as if she were her own daughter. "You came! You came!"

Eric felt his eyes well up with tears. Seeing Keeah older, and the queen, made him deeply happy, as if he knew it should be so. It also made him wonder for a moment about himself, the one who had seen Ko's terrible victory.

Had he died in battle, too? Which one — the third, the seventh? Or was he at home in the Upper World, a man sixty-plus years old? And not a part of Droon anymore? He shook his head to wipe that thought away.

"Why are you sharpening this blade?" he asked the queen. "Who are you going to fight? Galen said the battle is over."

Queen Keeah stood up and took the sword in her hand. "There is one fight I will never give up fighting." She stared deeply into Eric's eyes. "The fight to free you."

Eric felt his heart quiver when he heard the words. "To free me? What do you mean?"

Max hobbled into the room. "Sensing that the city would fall, Galen defied danger. Oh, he was brave! He stole into the city at night to retrieve the Moon Medallion his mother made in her sacred grove. He said that if ever there was a time we needed it, now was that time. He was nearly free when a troop of vicious beasts descended on him. Boldly and bravely, Eric came to rescue him. Galen got free. But poor Prince Eric . . ."

"Prince?" said Eric. "I'm a prince?"

Queen Keeah's eyes grew moist. She nodded. "He — you — lies imprisoned in the deepest levels of what was once Jaffa City. I am going tonight to try once again to rescue him."

Eric couldn't believe what he was hearing.

"But, Princess, how?" asked Captain Bludge. "All the beasts have gathered for the destruction of the Ring of Midnight.

Even with us at your side, we are still fewer than ten in number."

Eric breathed deeply. He turned to the others and smiled. "If I remember, being totally outnumbered is pretty much our style."

"That's the Eric I remember!" said the queen.

"Hoo-hoo!" crowed Galen, jumping like a much younger man. "People, we're in business again! Captain Bludge! Ninns! There is hope once more. Ready yourselves!"

Bludge gargled a Ninn laugh. "We have been ready for years!"

Eric's breath caught in his throat.

He looked at Max and Galen.

He turned to Keeah and the queen.

"To Jaffa City!" he declared.

# Ten.

# Under the Black Palace

Too old and frail to fight, Galen and Max waved from the cottage door as Eric, Captain Bludge, five Ninn warriors, and two Keeahs made their way swiftly to the edge of the Farne Woods.

Taking cover behind a large bush, the little band stared out across an open plain to Jaffa City.

Eric swallowed back a gasp as he again glimpsed the once-pink walls charred black from fire. Armed gray-furred beasts paraded along the top, while from the sunken palace dome a powerful searchlight beamed back and forth across the open ground around the city.

"We'll never get to the walls without being seen," said the queen. "The distance is short, but there are only seconds between each sweeping of that light."

"If only the woods were closer to the city," said Eric.

The Ninn commander made a sound like a laugh. "Junior Prince Eric! What a good idea!"

He turned to him. "Um . . . it is?"

"Bring the woods closer!" said Bludge. "We hide behind branches and move forward. When the light passes over us, we stop. Yard by yard, step-by-step, we reach the walls. This is what you meant, right?"

Eric's heart skipped a beat. "Sure,

that's what I meant. Let's dress up . . . as plants!"

The little troop gathered fallen branches, hid behind them, and moved over the open ground toward the walls. When the beasts' spotlight swept toward them, they stopped.

The moment they were hidden by darkness again, they moved on. Soon the troop arrived at the foot of the city walls.

Keeah remembered that since Jaffa City was on the water, there were tunnels beneath the city that allowed the tides to ebb and flow under it.

The queen smiled. "I know the nearest tunnel. It will take us to the lowest passages under the palace."

Five minutes later, the little group had slipped under the walls and entered a world of crumbling black stone. The

hallways twisted oddly, creating a terrifying maze that Keeah hardly recognized as
her home.

They entered one passage that took
them nearly up to ground level before
slanting down again.

Through cracks in the passage walls,
Eric glimpsed the courtyard outside the
palace. It was filled with beasts that were
erecting a column made of giant trees
hooped together by thick bands of iron.

"What is that?" he asked.

The queen paused. "It looks like a
handle."

"For what?"

"A big hammer?" she suggested.

"Why do the beasts want such a huge
hammer?" Keeah asked.

The queen gulped. "Maybe to break
something with?"

*Errrch!* Inch by inch, the beasts lifted the giant hammer into an upright position over the courtyard.

"We need to move on," said Bludge. "Prince Eric lies in the lowest level of the palace."

As they pressed deeper through the passages, Eric wondered what his older self might look like. He knew he would be old. After all, he was not a *droomar* as Keeah was. Nor was he a wizard like Sparr or Urik or Galen. If he ever was such a wizard, he certainly wasn't anymore. He would have aged like Max had aged. To say nothing of having lived in a dungeon for so long!

Would they even find him alive?

"Footsteps," said the princess.

Queen Keeah whirled around. A troop of scale-covered beasts with horned heads hissed when they saw the friends.

"Spies! Get them!" their leader snarled. "Bring them to Ko —"

Queen Keeah did not hesitate. Saying nothing, she flashed her sharpened saber in the dark, and the beasts fell back, howling.

A moment later, an alarm sounded in the passages.

"They know about us now," said Eric.

"We Ninns will guard the way," said Bludge. "Do what you must do. Go. Go!"

There was no time to argue. The footsteps returned, and there were many more of them.

Wishing the Ninns good luck, the queen, Keeah, and Eric raced deeper and deeper through the black passages. The two wizards ran ahead into the dark, guided by the queen's gleaming saber. Eric hurried after them, only to find himself lost at a place where the passage split in two.

He stopped and whispered as loudly as he could into one passage, then the other.

"Keeah? Keeah!"

There was no answer from either tunnel.

"Uh-oh," he said to himself.

He moved tentatively into one tunnel, went around a sharp corner, and found a torch lying on the floor. When he picked it up and held it high, he was stunned to see what he thought was a face hovering in the darkness ahead.

He froze.

"Hello?"

"Hey. How's it going?"

Eric gulped. "Who's . . . there . . . ?"

The face approached. It was a young-ish woman with a thicket of thorns for hair. Her face bore a green tint.

"Salamandra!" said Eric, holding the torch to one side. "What are you doing

here? How did you even get here? Wait . . .
is the Portal coming? Are you coming to
get us? Do we have to go back to the present? We only have the Twilight Star. Don't
we need the Ring of Midnight —"

"Whoa, Eric!" the thorn queen said.
"One question at a time. A girl can only
take so much. Besides, I'm not even here."

He stepped back. "What do you mean?"

She gave him a look. "Think, Eric. I'm
not here. If I'm not here, I must be somewhere else. If I'm somewhere else, then
who are you talking to?"

He stared at her green face. She looked
annoyed at him. He gasped suddenly.

"A . . . a . . ."

"Say it. . . ."

"A . . . *vision*?"

"Bingo!" said Salamandra with a smile
that lit up her face. "So, good job, Eric
Hinkle. Now, find the prince. He's thataway."

She pointed over her shoulder. "I'll take my staff now. It goes with my hair."

"Your staff?" Eric looked at the torch in his hand only to find that it was not a torch at all. It was Salamandra's magical staff, glowing in its own thorny fire.

She snatched it from him, then faded from the passage as if she were nothing more than smoke.

Eric stared at the hand that had held the staff, then blinked into the darkness ahead, dumbfounded. "What just happened here? The last time I held Salamandra's staff, it took all my powers away —"

He stopped. At just that moment, he heard the sound of stone scraping on stone. Shaking his head to clear it, he repeated the queen's words.

"Thataway? So okay. I'll go thataway!"

Eric stumbled ahead in the dark until he

found an iron door set into the stone. A heavy bar was laid over its frame. With all his might, he lifted up the bar and dropped it to the floor with a clang.

He pulled the door open. Inside was a small stone cell. Hunched over, bound in an intricate web of thick chains, was the shape of a man. He was digging at the floor.

"Uh . . . me?" said Eric.

The man raised his head from his work and turned slowly to the doorway.

Eric saw his future self.

He was young! He looked perhaps twenty years old, as old as Queen Keeah. Though this was five decades in the future, it was the same face — *his* face — only a few years older!

"Prince Eric," said Eric, "we've come to free you!"

The prince beamed. "I can't believe it. It's just as Galen hoped. You! I mean, me! Eric!"

All at once, the two Keeahs ran in.

Eric and Princess Keeah watched as the queen rushed to the prince, tore away his chains with a single blast of sparks, and raised him from the floor. Then she hugged him tightly. It was an embrace that neither seemed to want to end.

Finally, though, the passages resounded with the sound of fighting.

"Captain Bludge is protecting us, but there are lots of beasts," said Keeah. "We need to get the Ring of Midnight and get out of here!"

Prince Eric nodded sharply. "Ko plans to destroy the Ring of Midnight at midnight tonight, when the moon is full."

"The hammer!" said Eric.

The prince nodded as he darted out into the passage. "Ko's hammer is loaded with the ancient dark magic of Goll. We have no time to lose."

While the Ninns held back the beasts, the prince, the queen, Keeah, and Eric raced through one narrow passage after another until they arrived on the edge of the court-yard.

It was filled with more roaring beasts than they could have imagined.

The giant hammer was upright now, poised over a flat stone disk. Barely visible on the disk was a silver ring the size of a bracelet. It was tied down like a victim at a stake.

"The Ring of Midnight!" said Eric.

"If that is destroyed," said the queen, "Ko will wage his final attack on Galen and surely defeat him."

The giant emperor stood before the

beasts and quieted their roar with his four hands. His twin horns spurted tall columns of green flame nearly as high as the dome itself.

"Beasts!" he boomed. "Five decades ago, we marched on Jaffa City and set it to the torch. It has taken all this time to find and destroy all the parts of the Moon Medallion that protected the city. Only the final part remains to be created. If I know Gethwing, he will find it. And if I know myself, I shall soon have it!"

The beasts roared wildly.

Eric held the Twilight Star in his hand. It burned like fire and ice at the same time.

"If only Galen were young enough to be with us now," said Prince Eric, glancing at the Star. "Only a son of Zara can unharness the Medallion or its parts. I'm not even a wizard. I lost my powers long ago."

*So,* thought Eric, *in this future, I never get my powers back.*

"Tonight," continued Ko, "we destroy the final vestiges of the rule of wizards. Tonight the Empire of Goll rises to its full glory!"

"I'll make my way to the hammer and try to snatch the Ring," said the prince. "Eric, stay in the shadows. We can't risk the Twilight Star being stolen, too. We must keep it safe."

"I'll do what I can," said Eric.

"Princess Keeah and I will blast the beasts and cover you, Prince Eric," said the queen with a smile. "Just don't get caught this time."

The prince smiled back. "Let me think about that. *Mmm . . .* okay!"

"Is the hammer ready?" shouted Ko.

"It is!" yelled a chorus of beasts.

Prince Eric nodded at the others. "And so am I. When Ko gives the order, we move!"

Eric watched his older self move quietly among the crowd of beasts and was proud to see how he had ended up. Prince Eric was nothing less than a hero, with or without wizard powers.

"Then let the hammer fall!" Ko boomed, and Prince Eric took off through the crowd. At the same time, the two Keeahs blasted the courtyard with purple sparks. The beasts howled and dived for cover.

Prince Eric was inches away from the Ring of Midnight when Ko spotted him and fired a bolt of black fire. The prince was hurled away into a crowd of angry beasts. They surrounded him and held him down.

"Noooo!" yelled the queen. Together

with Keeah's sparks she repelled Ko's terrifying blasts and sent him leaping away.

But the giant hammer had already started to fall.

"Save the Ring!" shouted Prince Eric as he struggled to get free of the beasts. "Eric — save the Ring!"

"Me?" Eric said from the shadows. "But what can I . . ?"

The Twilight Star burned in his hand hotter than ever. He felt his head grow hazy. His heart thumped as he saw the hammer falling, falling. All of a sudden Eric found himself running as swiftly as he could toward the Ring of Midnight. But he wasn't fast enough. The hammer was nearly down.

"Nooooo!" he cried. He reached toward the Ring with his free hand, then felt suddenly as if his hand were being yanked through the air. His feet left the ground. He flew like a rocket across the courtyard, snatching the silver Ring of Midnight from the stone an instant before the hammer crashed down.

"What? What —"

He had flown! He had flown!

Beasts were on him in a second, but he flashed around, with the Star in one hand and the Ring in the other. Silver sparks burst from his fingertips. His sizzling spray hurled the beasts back into the crowd.

"My powers!" Eric cried. "My powers! They're back!"

"And so are mine!" shouted Prince Eric as his fingertips flashed. He blasted his way free.

All the beasts charged the four friends. Then came the gargling sound of Ninn laughter as Captain Bludge and his band leaped into the courtyard with blades flashing. With a cheer, the four friends sent silver and purple streams of sparks at the beasts until the terrifying creatures were all forced to run for safety.

That was when a giant silver web fell over the beasts, and Max and Galen appeared on the city wall.

"Well, what did you expect?" said the wizard. "We couldn't miss *all* the fun!"

"Not a chance," chirped Max. "Spider trolls were born for adventure!"

With that, the wizard and Max joined the Ninns, and the courtyard erupted into a mad scene of sparks and webs and growling and running. It was a terrible din, but above it all came the sound of a storm.

"The Portal of Ages!" said Keeah. "Eric, it's coming for us. We have the pieces of the Medallion. We need to go back to the present!"

"When you get back to the present," said Galen, "remember one thing: Meet me at the gates to Jaffa City! Meet me there!"

"Go!" said Prince Eric, his fingers sparking. "Save the future. Save Droon!"

The two children hugged their older selves, leaped up into the storm, and went spinning away — far away — and half a century into the past.

# Eleven

# The Magic of the Moon

Eric and Keeah kept their hands locked together as the ferocious winds of time tried to drive them apart.

"Something's coming at us!" Keeah yelled.

"Whoooooooa!" cried a familiar voice.

"Something's coming at us, all right!" said Eric. "Something called . . . Neal!"

Neal hurtled through the Portal at terrifying speed while Julie clung to his feet.

Reaching out with their hands, the four friends met in the swirling Portal. Together they bobbled and wobbled through the air, spun around a dozen times, then began to fall.

"Get ready to — ahhhh!" screamed Neal.

*PLOP!*

The four friends landed together as softly as they had before. Bouncing to their feet, they found themselves before the gates of Jaffa City. To Eric's and Keeah's relief, the city gleamed and glittered as it always had.

"Have we got stories for you!" said Julie.

"That makes four of us!" said Keeah.

"We were in the Upper World," said Neal. "We saw Zara and Urik in the past! We got the base of the Medallion and the Pearl Sea!"

"We saw Sparr in the future!" said Eric.

"And we have the Ring of Midnight and Sparr's Twilight Star!"

"Uh . . . guys," said Julie. "Take a look."

In the east was a moving cloud of dust.

The children knew what it was.

Wielding torches and spears, Ko's armies of beasts were marching toward Jaffa City from the distant Dark Lands.

"This is why we're here, after all," said Keeah.

Julie turned to her friends. "I never thought I'd say this, guys, but I'm glad the beasts are on the march. It means they haven't taken over yet. We came before the battle started. We still have time."

"But not much. They're really moving," said Neal. "Come on, Galen, wherever you are. Pedal to the metal!"

Eric felt his heart pound.

The Twilight Star in his hand pulsed

with waves of cold and heat. Julie held the base of the Medallion. Its markings sparkled in the setting sun. Keeah wore the Ring of Midnight like a bracelet on her wrist. Neal had set the Pearl Sea as a jewel in his turban. Its hazy insides moved like drifting clouds.

Looking east, Eric saw Ko's armies spilling toward them like a black cloud. The emperor marched at their head, his twin horns spouting green flames.

Looking south, Eric watched the mounted forces of King Zello and Queen Relna gallop toward them at full speed. The king and queen were carrying Droon's banners high.

Many miles away on a mountain peak in Panjibarrh, Salamandra stood, her thorn staff burning with a bright flame.

*Thank you!* Eric said silently to her.

*Eh, don't mention it,* was her response.

For Eric to have his powers back was a feeling more welcome than he could ever have imagined.

All of a sudden — *whoosh!* — a flying carpet landed nearby. Galen and Max jumped off and ran to the children.

"Ah, just as I had hoped," said Galen. "Do you have the Medallion and its parts?"

"We do," said Keeah. "But how will we stop Ko?"

"It took me fifty years to figure that out," said the wizard. "And yet it came to me in an instant. We will trick the emperor as he has never been tricked before."

"I like tricks," said Neal. "Especially when they're played on evil beast emperors."

"Just how I feel," said Galen, turning to the approaching armies. "Now, I would say good luck in the coming battle, but we need more than luck, and I'm not sure that what happens here will actually be a battle. But give me the items, stand back, and behold real power!"

As the beasts marched ever closer, Julie handed Galen the base of the Medallion. When the wizard took the silver disk in his hands and kissed it, it chimed as if it were a bell.

"The foundation of my mother's magic," he said. "Next . . ."

Keeah slipped the Ring of Midnight from her wrist and gave it to him. Galen smiled at his own creation. When he locked it into place, it began to hum. "Next."

Neal plucked Urik's Pearl Sea from the folds of his turban. Galen took it and placed it in the center of the Medallion. It beamed as if lit from inside.

When it came time for Eric to hand over the Twilight Star, his fingers burned as they never had before. "Zara helped Sparr make this."

Letting go of the Star made Eric's chest ache, as he had so often ached when he spoke Zara's name. He also grieved for the loss of Sparr and could not forget the sight of the sorcerer falling, falling into the black abyss.

Galen held the Star high before attaching it to the center of the disk.

"Now the Medallion is complete."

He walked solemnly away from the children and turned his face to the skies.

The thundering armies marched closer.

When Galen murmured a word, the Twilight Star began to spin. Light shot from its points and from the Pearl Sea, while the

Ring of Midnight hummed and the whole Medallion beamed.

As they watched, a sudden dark wind whirled out from the Medallion's center and roared across the plains. It completely hid the great royal city and the friends from the approaching armies.

"Master!" cried Max. "What's happening?"

Galen smiled when he raised his arms.

"Do not worry, my valiant friend," he said. "All is safe. Now behold Queen Zara's legacy as we have never witnessed it before!"

Whether the moon overhead chose that moment to reveal itself, or whether the Medallion summoned it from the dark sky, the children could not tell.

All they knew was that a column of brilliant silver light shot between the

Moon Medallion and its namesake in the sky. It pulsed and vibrated. It hummed a note of increasing pitch that grew louder and louder.

Eric's ears perked up as Galen whispered words that he read on the Medallion.

*I know those words!*

Brilliant light shot out in every direction, then the ground flattened in front of them like dough under an enormous rolling pin.

The plain filled with water that immediately turned to frosty blue ice.

Then — *whooom!* — the earth cracked open along the edges of the frozen lake, and light burst up from it. A pink wall exploded upward from below. Another wall emerged, then another. Pink and tall, the walls were bathed in silver light.

"It looks like Jaffa City!" said Keeah.

Towers came next, here, there, everywhere. Then the great golden dome of the palace appeared over them all.

Galen smiled. "An illusion caused by the Medallion's magic. We shall defend not the real city but these imaginary walls! Thus does my mother set a trap for Ko, whose strength of will and the power of his dark desires are not matched by his intelligence."

Neal snickered. "Yeah. His parents probably named him Ko because they knew he wouldn't be able to spell a longer name."

"Ah, but the emperor is a brute who stops at nothing," said the wizard. "We must put up a fight or he will sense a trap, and Droon will truly be lost!"

At that, Galen waved his hand over the Medallion, the dark wind dissolved around the friends, and the moving sea of enemy torches came within striking distance of the city.

"To your places, everyone!" shouted Max.

Galen drew a deep breath. Keeah clasped Eric by the hand, then let go and aimed her hands at the beast armies.

Ko was first over the hill. He stopped when he beheld what he believed was Jaffa City. He threw his massive arms out on both sides, and squads of enormous lion-shaped beasts and many-tusked dragon warriors flanked him. The ground shuddered as the first wave of beasts rose over the ridge. The line of his armies extended across the plains for miles in each direction. With one stomp, they stood at attention, and the night went still.

"Oh, boy, oh, boy . . ." Neal grumbled.

"Are we ready? Yes?" said Galen, echoing Sparr's words at the forge.

"Yes!" said Eric.

"Yes," they all cried.

Ko cast a smoldering glance from one side to the other, then howled. "Burn Jatta City!"

And the battle began.

# Twelve

# A Very Good Thing

The battle before the gates was an inferno of clashing iron and steel and wood and the sizzling of wizard staffs.

Eric, Keeah, Neal, and Julie were like their own little army. On Eric's signal, they charged the beasts from the side. Blasting and flying, they managed to send hundreds in retreat. Meanwhile, great lion-headed warriors circled behind the children to surprise them. Only Neal's genie sense alerted them in time to run to safety.

Galen waded into the attacking forces, his sparking staff flying in every direction at once, while Max, Zello, and Relna became a wall of fury, driving the beasts backward.

In this way, everyone fought to keep Ko from the gates of the city.

But the beasts numbered in the thousands. They poured across the plains in wave after wave. They pushed their way yard by yard to the city gates. Finally, they wheeled forward a giant battering ram. Its head was a great iron bust of Ko. Its horns spouted their own fire.

"Pull back, everyone. We have lost the city!" cried Galen.

At the wizard's command, the children and all the king's troops fell back behind a high ridge on the southern plains.

Ko bellowed, "They have retreated! The city is ours! Burn it! Burn it to the ground!"

*Wham-wham-wham!* The battering ram pummeled the gates time and time again. On the tenth blow, the gates split apart, and the beasts flooded in, torches raised high.

Galen crowed from the top of the ridge, "And now we have them!"

With a twist of the Medallion, the moon fell behind a black cloud as swiftly as if a switch had shut it off. The silver light vanished in a twinkling, and so did the imaginary city itself.

Towers, walls, bridges, the great dome — the entire city collapsed upon itself, dissolving like snow on a summer day. The lake reappeared underneath, unfroze, and the beasts dropped into the water, splashing wildly up to their chins.

Their torches hissed and fizzled in the water. The beasts erupted in shouts and cries that echoed across the plains all the way to the Dark Lands.

"I always knew beasts didn't like baths!" said Neal.

Ko and his army floundered in the water. They were soon surrounded by the great forces of King Zello's royal army.

"Ko, you have not conquered Jaffa City at all!" cried the king. "Our towers are as stately and beautiful as ever! Galen, show him!"

With a laugh, Galen waved the Medallion, and the real Jaffa City glistened in front of them, as splendid and majestic as its first day.

Ko stomped to the shore, the green flame of his horns sputtering. "Galen!" he boomed. "This battle is not over!"

"It is, actually," said Eric, his heart thumping with pride. "The Moon Medallion will always overpower you. It did today. It will in the future! Believe me, I know!"

"Now, be gone, defeated emperor of beasts!" shouted Galen. "Before our true power falls on you!"

Ko howled. "You've not seen the last – "

"Blah, blah, blah," said Neal.

"We shall rise again and —"

"Oh, you *shall* rise!" chirped Max. "Didn't you know about the underground spring? Well, get ready, because here it comes!"

All at once, the lake exploded into an enormous spout of water. It hurled Ko and his beast army across the plains toward the Dark Lands until they could be seen no more. With that, the water vanished, and the plains rolled on and on as peacefully as they ever had.

For a long time afterward, Eric, Julie, Keeah, and Neal stood, staring out at the beautiful landscape of Droon.

"I wish somebody could tell me what actually happened today," said Eric. "And what exactly we did."

"You saved Droon," said Queen Relna, riding up to them with King Zello by her side.

"I sense a new beginning for Droon," said the wizard, smiling from ear to ear. "We have only begun to discover what real powers lie in the Moon Medallion —"

"Hold on," said Max. "Look at that!"

The sky darkened with a sudden funnel of spinning air. It touched down with a tremendous crash, then vanished.

A moment later, Salamandra appeared, cradling her starfox in one hand and her thorn staff in the other. "Hey," she said, "looks like you've done pretty well. But no, no, don't thank me. I guess I'm just a generous sorceress."

"You helped us today," said Eric. "You helped me today. Lots."

Salamandra shrugged. "It's mutual."

"What's ahead for us now?" asked Max.

"One secret at a time, shorty," said Salamandra with a laugh. "First, you gotta give up the Medallion. You know its pieces have to go back to where you borrowed them from."

Galen grumbled. But he knew she was right and did as she asked.

Salamandra tossed the four parts of the Medallion into the air. The Portal appeared and sucked them away — the base of the Medallion to Zara to begin its long journey through time, the Pearl Sea to Urik in the apple grove, the Ring of Midnight to the time and place it was last seen, and the Twilight Star to the future when Sparr would create it.

But no sooner had the parts vanished than they reappeared in Galen's hand — all except for the Twilight Star, which had not yet been made.

"They have come full circle!" said Max.

"We'll need the Star to battle Ko again," said Keeah.

"And . . . you . . . shall . . . have . . . it!" said a sudden voice.

Everyone turned to see a lone figure stumbling toward them in short, uneven steps.

It was a tall, thin man in a tattered cloak. His eyes were black, his face darkened by smoke and dirt. The edges of his cloak were frayed and glowed like embers. And his hair was as silver as the moonlight.

"Oh, my gosh! It's Sparr! From the future!" said Eric, running to him.

Hearing his name, the sorcerer staggered over the ground toward them.

Eric held his arm and helped him forward. "You fought Gethwing in the Underworld," he said. "You fell thousands of feet. I was sure you died in that fall."

"Perhaps I did," said the sorcerer. His voice was faint, weak, barely a whisper.

"You should rest," said Galen, taking his other arm.

"No . . . no . . ." he answered, turning toward his brother and handing him the Twilight Star, but still moving forward.

Eric thought it was odd how Sparr looked past Galen when he spoke to him. As if he didn't know him. Sparr stumbled on a stone, but caught himself and kept walking.

Eric felt his chest ache as never before. He realized that Sparr couldn't see Galen.

He couldn't see anyone or anything.

Sparr was blind.

"Oh, my gosh!" said Eric. "Your eyes —"

Sparr took a step, then faltered. "I go north across the plains."

Galen shook his head. "No, no. You cannot have returned to us only to leave again. You cannot. What is in the north?"

"Our mother is there," Sparr said.

Galen hung his head. "Brother, she is not. The *droomar* buried her. Long ago. In Bangledorn Forest. You remember. . . ."

"I . . . I know she is there in the north," Sparr said. "She is calling me. I hear her voice in my mind." He moved away from them.

"But there are rivers and mountains and forests every inch of the way," said Eric. "You can't see where you're going!"

Sparr turned vaguely to him. "The mind sees, too, Eric Hinkle. It will guide me. Know, too, that Gethwing is not gone. I see in my mind his shadow lurking. He nurses his wounds. He will return. Until then, the silver waters of the north call me. My race is not yet run, my quest continues, my journey calls me forward. I go."

He touched Eric's arm once more for support and gripped it tightly. He patted Galen's hand, which still clung to him, then removed it. "I go. Kem, my friend! Lead me!"

Grumbling and barking, Sparr's two-headed pet tramped up over the ridge, shook himself, and took his place next to Sparr.

The sorcerer paused. "But . . . let me touch the Star once more."

Galen guided the sorcerer's white hand to it, and the man's face shone in its glow as his fingers played over its markings.

"The Medallion's great trial has not yet come," Sparr said. "In the meantime, keep it secret. Keep it safe. Until we meet again."

Eric was on the verge of tears. "Will you come back?"

Sparr turned his face to Eric. "That depends."

"On what?"

"On whether there is anywhere to come back to."

Kem nudged the sorcerer along tentatively, whispering to his master. And they made their way slowly toward the vast reaches of the frozen north. Soon Sparr and his dog disappeared over the hills and could be seen no more.

Eric felt a pain in his chest when he imagined the two alone on their long, dark journey, searching for someone who could not possibly be alive. He thought of Sparr grasping his arm for support, then wondered if that support was not so much for the wounded man as it was for Eric himself.

In that moment, he felt very close to the old sorcerer.

Galen watched his brother go, then attached the Twilight Star to the Medallion. "We have the whole Medallion now," he said. "Will we ever have the brothers together — Sparr, Urik, and myself — as we were so long ago?"

No one answered the wizard.

No one *could* answer him.

"Oh, that reminds me," said Salamandra. "Eric, in case you forgot. *Reki-ur-set!*"

"Okay, now what does that mean?" Eric demanded. "You always say it, then you go."

Salamandra took a single step backward, and the Portal reappeared. "What a good idea! Besides, you've got your powers. You'll figure it out. Buh-bye!"

With a brief wave, Salamandra jumped into the whirling Portal and was gone.

In the same moment — *whoosh!* — the rainbow staircase materialized before them, glistening in the silver moonlight from above.

"What a day!" said Julie. "I feel as if we've been everywhere and done everything."

"Time for home," said Neal, removing his turban. "Time to be normal again."

Eric looked down at his fingers. They sparked softly. He smiled. "Being normal used to be easy for me. Not anymore. I'm glad."

"Children, come back soon," said Galen. "Something tells me that before long there will be a new quest for all of us. There are many more secrets to discover!"

As the three friends ran up the rainbow stairs, Zello and Relna led their Droon friends back into Jaffa City — the *real* Jaffa City.

Night fell over Droon. All was quiet.

All was quiet in Droon, but every inch of his way home, Eric's mind reeled with questions.

Was Salamandra good or bad? What did *Reki-ur-set* mean? How did Urik's Pearl Sea end up at his house? How did a book that seemed to be written by Urik ever end up at his town library? Why was he himself so young in the future? Would they see Sparr again? Would he be as old as they had just seen him?

The questions didn't stop, and he had no answers for any of them.

But if these secrets were still in shadow, Eric felt he was moving closer to solving them.

After Neal and Julie said good-bye on his back step, Eric went upstairs and sat staring out his bedroom window until midnight.

The moon was a silver disk beaming over his yard, through the apple trees by his house, and onto his bed. Nearby hung a single star twinkling brightly. Far below and two towns away stood the sea, its surface pearly in the moonlight.

Eric breathed in the warm air.

Mysteries, secrets, puzzles were everywhere. Now as the moonlight shone its silver light onto his world, he knew one thing. And it was a good thing. It was a very good thing.

His powers were finally back.

# About the Author

Tony Abbott is the author of more than sixty funny novels for young readers, including the popular *Danger Guys* books and The *Weird Zone* series, as well as *Kringle*, his hardcover novel from Scholastic Press. Since childhood he has been drawn to stories that challenge the imagination, and, like Eric, Julie, and Neal, he often dreamed of finding doors that open to other worlds. Now that he is older — though not quite as old as Galen Longbeard — he believes he may have found some of those doors. They are called books. Tony Abbott was born in Ohio and now lives with his wife and two daughters in Connecticut.

For more information about Tony Abbott and the continuing saga of Droon, visit www.tonyabbottbooks.com.

# THE SECRETS OF DROON

By Tony Abbott

**Read them all!**

## Under the stairs, a magical world awaits you!

- ❏ #1: The Hidden Stairs and the Magic Carpet
- ❏ #2: Journey to the Volcano Palace
- ❏ #3: The Mysterious Island
- ❏ #4: City in the Clouds
- ❏ #5: The Great Ice Battle
- ❏ #6: The Sleeping Giant of Goll
- ❏ #7: Into the Land of the Lost
- ❏ #8: The Golden Wasp
- ❏ #9: The Tower of the Elf King
- ❏ #10: Quest for the Queen
- ❏ #11: The Hawk Bandits of Tarkoom
- ❏ #12: Under the Serpent Sea
- ❏ #13: The Mask of Maliban
- ❏ #14: Voyage of the *Jaffa Wind*
- ❏ #15: The Moon Scroll
- ❏ #16: The Knights of Silversnow
- ❏ #17: Dream Thief
- ❏ #18: Search for the Dragon Ship
- ❏ #19: The Coiled Viper
- ❏ #20: In the Ice Caves of Krog
- ❏ #21: Flight of the Genie
- ❏ #22: The Isle of Mists
- ❏ #23: The Fortress of the Treasure Queen
- ❏ #24: The Race to Doobesh
- ❏ #25: The Riddle of Zorfendorf Castle
- ❏ #26: The Moon Dragon
- ❏ #27: The Chariot of Queen Zara
- ❏ #28: In the Shadow of Goll
- ❏ #29: Pirates of the Purple Dawn
- ❏ #30: Escape from Jabar-Loo
- ❏ #31: Queen of Shadowthorn

---

- ❏ Special Edition #1: The Magic Escapes
- ❏ Special Edition #2: Wizard or Witch?
- ❏ Special Edition #3: Voyagers of the Silver Sand
- ❏ Special Edition #4: Sorcerer

Over 6.7 million copies sold!

📖 SCHOLASTIC

**www.scholastic.com/droon**

DroonBL1

# Out of the darkness, a hero will rise.